About *The Late Worm*

A fourth collection of head-scratching nanopieces: funny, horrifying, bemusing, and completely unclassifiable. This book is absolutely unique except for its three predecessors and any other books I decide to write (plus the minutes from that one unusual town council meeting in Idaho).

Learn why Ahab missed, how to avoid being labeled a forester, why it's important to show up very very late, and how to avoid being spontaneously spousified. Everything you need in order to live a short, cautionary tale of a life is presented here in eyepopping Palatino ten-point. For one millionth the price of a college education, you can learn a billionth as much.

Other Books

The Tale of Rin: Protege (*novel*): Just because Rin is indestructible doesn't mean she can't be hurt. On her quest to remedy an ancient sin, a single act of casual cruelty sets off an avalanche of events which threaten to destroy everything. Rin must rein in her assistant, a man of fierce attachment and questionable conviction, while avoiding a devious ex-husband who will stop at nothing to reclaim her. In the balance lies her heart and the fate of the world.

PACE (*novel*): A mysterious Front, originating in Scotland and slowly expanding outward, threatens humanity's existence. In defiance of the known laws of physics, it only kills humans and is otherwise undetectable. Panic-stricken nations struggle against both the advancing menace and a tide of civil unrest. Desperate individuals must find their own paths and find them quickly. Mankind has only a few years to pool its rapidly dwindling resources and save itself from extinction.

The Delivery (*novella*): Wilbur is an unassuming little man living an unassuming little life. He and his wife have a stereotypical 1950s existence but in modern America. One day, he arrives home to discover a mysterious crate. His attempts to deal with it trigger an escalating series of absurdities that strain his marriage, leave the couple's life in tatters, and lead him to question his place in the world.

The Man Who Stands in Line (*flash fiction*): Killer flies, amorous dinosaurs, angry buildings, and one very large fish — all in a single volume. A surreal and humorous view of the usual questions of self, purpose, and society. This quirky collection of flash fiction, vignettes, and poetry is variously absurd, dark, and comic. *Also available as an audiobook.*

The Way Around (*flash fiction*): More absurd, horrifying, and downright inexplicable shorts. Included are such soon-to-be classics as Buzz-Saw Bob, the sport of pendulum watching, yet another secret to ultimate success, the art of gasping, a neighbor who is definitely not Mr. Rogers, and Buddha's morning commute. *Also available as an audiobook.*

The Last Cloud (*flash fiction*): Meet the superhero Spleen Squeezer, discover the true story of Eden, and travel to the safest city in the world in this 3rd collection of unclassifiable ultra-short pieces. But wait, there's MORE!!!! Learn the danger of having ears, the importance of being unlikable, and how to achieve quality as an executioner. *Also available as an audiobook.*

The Below (*novella*): When hard-nosed lawyer Beth follows a strange man into a hidden cave, she finds herself in a massive subterranean world known as "The Below". As she learns about this secret place and grows closer to her guide, she discovers a surprising side to herself. But all is not as it seems, and the apparent tranquility may obscure a darker truth.

All are available as ***paperbacks*** *through* ***Amazon***, ***Barnes & Noble***, ***Waterstones***, *and other bookstores in the U.S. and internationally, as* ***Kindle ebooks*** *through* ***Amazon***, *and (where applicable) as* ***audiobooks*** *through* ***Audible***.

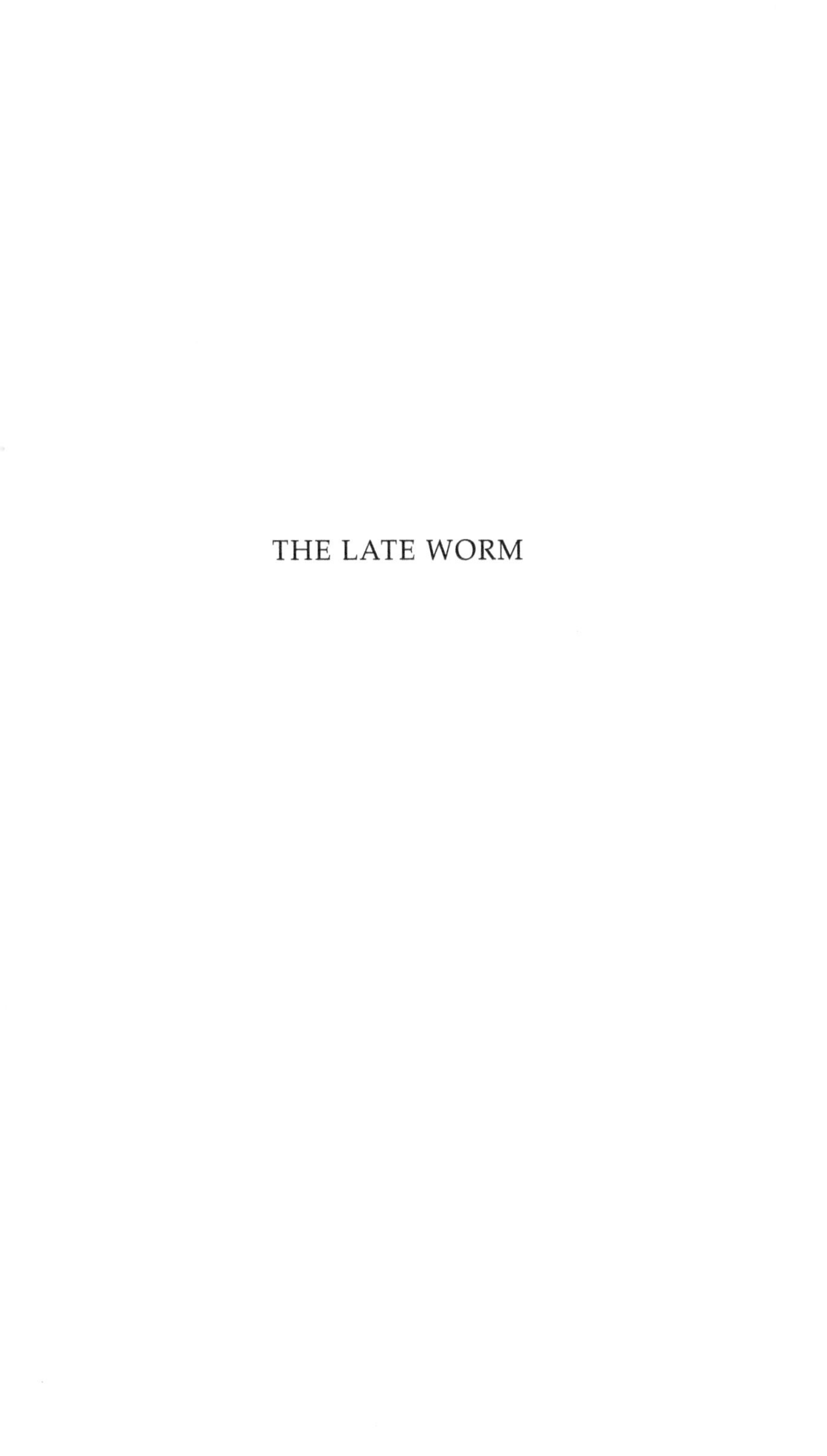

THE LATE WORM

THE LATE WORM

A Fourth
Pretentious Collection of Very Short Works

by

K.M. Halpern

εpsilon Books

ISBN-13 (paperback): 978-1-945671-13-5

ISBN-13 (ebook): 978-1-945671-14-2

Library of Congress Control Number: 2021919981

Published by Epsilon Books

Printed in the United States of America

Cover Art by Richie Montgomery

First Edition

CONTENTS

Miscreance

It is a strange form of vandalism that we must contend with these days.

The youths emerge at night, some gently lowering themselves from windows, others tiptoeing past sleeping parents. One glares at an awakened sibling. The child shudders and closes its eyes. It will say nothing. Perhaps the parents also are awake. They too will say nothing. Whether from fear or shame, there is nothing to be said.

The gang soon gathers in an abandoned yard, each with a little bundle of trouble. The tools of the trade. One rolls his eyes in affected boredom, another dangles his lanky limbs with practiced insouciance. Two girls giggle, casting glances at a nervous boy. It is his first time. He is unsure whether their eyes invite or mock him. They too are unsure.

Soon the time has come. The leader of the leaderless group gives a signal. It is the signal that the time has come. It is the signal to cause trouble. To reject civilization and kinship and decency and law. To embrace not the camaraderie of the group, but the rebellion of the self. To do what is forbidden them, to do what is dangerous, to do what is taboo. It is time to do society harm.

The youths dash through the streets, some skipping, some sauntering, some weaving to and fro. There is nobody out this late, and anyone who was has hidden themselves. Who dares test what these troublesome youths are capable of?

Finally, they reach their destination. This is where trouble will be made. It is a place worthy of trouble. It is where they sit all day, being told what to do and what not to do, being taught what others think they should know, think they must hear. They hate it. They hate those others. This is the right place for the trouble they will cause. It is the only place for the trouble they will cause.

With a scowl, each clambers over the flimsy metal fence of the schoolyard. For the first time, they appear orderly, a tidy little row of soldiers. One quietly makes his way around back and produces a key. It is best not to wonder how he came by such a key. A moment passes, then another. His companions grow restless. They no longer are tidy little soldiers. One rolls his eyes, another dangles his lanky limbs, and two girls giggle.

A face appears behind the front doors, and they spring open. The horde pours in, invading, infecting. They riot through the halls. The school is theirs. No teachers, no hall monitors, no principal. Nobody to tell them what to do, what not to do. No goody two-shoes classmates, eager to tattle that they did what they must not or did not do what they must.

They can do what they will, and nobody will stop them. Nobody will know. The day will be bearable, remembering what they did at night. What they had.

This brings them together. This common purpose, this common lack of purpose. One day, they will reminisce. They will laugh about these times. As long as they are not caught. It would be bad to be caught. Especially for troublesome youths. There would be no reminiscences or laughter. Just faint wistful smiles. Or perhaps frowns. Grownups never smile. They do not know how.

They must never speak of this. It irks them that there is one more thing they must not do. A thing they created. The moment passes, the feeling passes. They are not grownups and never will be. They will be what they wish. Something else.

They arrive at the scene of the crime. Each sits in the proper seat, scoffs at what is written on the board. Residue from the daytime that has no place in their world. One moves to erase it, but another shakes his head. Somebody could notice. That would make trouble for them, and they only wish to make trouble for others.

The moment has arrived. Finally, but too soon. The air is thick and silent. They brace with anticipation. It is always new, always thrilling. Each opens the little bundle. A pen, some paper, a book.

They study through the night.

A strange form of vandalism indeed.

Sarcastic Sarcophagus

Sarcastic Sarcophagus, why are you so difficult to open?

If I were easy to open, people would rob me.

That isn't sarcastic. Your name is misleading.

How can you be misled by an inanimate container? I cannot lead you anywhere, so how can I mislead you?

That's not sarcasm either.

Nobody claimed it was, because there is nobody.

Can't you at least try?

There is no me to try. There is no you either.

Why do you say that? I'm right here.

Why would the living be inside a sarcophagus?

Well, to rob you. But first I'd have to get in.

Look around.

I thought I could not open you.

You could not, and you did not.

Then how did I get in?

You've been here all along but did not know it.

I don't find this very funny.

You weren't meant to find it funny. I'm the sarcastic sarcophagus.

That wasn't sarcastic either.

Only because you're not trying.

Don't Do It

Don't do it!

Sure, it's tempting to do it. Not doing it makes things inconvenient and expensive and unpleasant. You want to do it. Everyone wants to do it. That's why you're not supposed to do it. That's why there are rules telling you not to do it.

Everyone does it. Everyone does it all the time, in every possible way, in plain sight of everyone else. Nobody ever gets in trouble. People grin, people wink, people laugh. Everyone does it. Why shouldn't everyone?

Don't do it!

You're not everyone. If *you* do it, you'll do it slightly wrong. You'll try your best, take every precaution, be extra courteous and careful and conscientious. But something will be off.

Maybe *that's* what will be off. Maybe you shouldn't be courteous or careful or conscientious. Who can tell? Only one thing is certain: *something* will be off.

People won't grin or wink or laugh. Everyone will stop and stare. Dogs will stop barking, cars will stop honking. There will be dead silence. Just you, caught red-handed, doing it. They will point, they will scowl. Nobody does that. Not what you did. Not the way you did it. Why *would* anyone?

Don't do it!

You will be punished. There will be no mercy, no compassion. Society has zero tolerance for what you did. It is offensive, indefensible, incomprehensible.

Nobody will speak on your behalf, lest they be drawn into your disgrace. You will stand alone, trembling and naked. You and judgment will be all that remains of your world.

They will make an example of you. An example of why not to do the thing you are not supposed to do. Others get away. Not you.

You do not know the right words, the right way to smile, the right way to defuse before the fuse is lit. Before everyone knows what you did and there is no running or hiding or laughing it off.

Others know the right words, the right way to smile. They have friends. Not your friends and not any old friends. The right friends. Friends who would speak on their behalf.

These others are the right sort. Everyone. Everyone but you. You are not the right sort, the sort that can get away with doing this thing.

Don't do it!

There will be no helping you, no saving you. It is for others to do this thing they are not meant to do. You are not others. You are not everyone. You will do it wrong. You *are* wrong. Pray the world doesn't notice. Perhaps it won't.

Unless you do it.

Little Emma

I

Little Emma was born shy.
The doctor said her health was weak.
She didn't speak and made no friends.
An episode left her wheelchair-bound.
She could not eat and made odd noises.
Her mother loved her and cared for her.
Sometimes she read stories to her.
The words were wrong, but this didn't matter.
At twelve, she lost her mother.
They said she had been crushed by a truck.
A worker brought her to an office.
Strangers took care of her.
They were paid some money.
She was not loved but was not harmed.

II

Doug loved the Lord but rarely spoke to him.
He lived in a small home.
When young, his wife had left him.
She did not say goodbye.
He often cooked pasta and ate alone.
The time for children had passed.
He liked dogs.
His mother died when he was forty-seven.
He taught school but was distracted.
To pass the time, he wrote essays.
Nobody read them.

I+II

Doug volunteered at the social office.
One day, he saw Emma being wheeled in.
He adopted her.
She was twenty, and he was fifty-five.
They went to the lake together.
They went to the park together.
He read to her, and she smiled.
She loved him as a father.
At thirty-six, she had a stroke.
He buried her.
Every year he visited her grave.
He wrote more essays.
Sometimes he mailed them to magazines.
None were published.
At sixty-nine, he died.
His essays were thrown away.

I-II

Doug once passed Emma on the street.
They did not notice one another.

I

At twenty, Emma was moved to a home.
The nurses washed and fed her.
Nobody talked to her or read to her.
In time, she forgot her name.
At forty-two, she had a seizure.
She no longer could see, and her arm hurt.
Eventually she died and was buried.
They wrote off the funeral expenses.

II

At fifty-eight, Doug lost his job.
He sold his house and moved.
While moving he fell.
The doctors cost money.
Soon he was poor.
At sixty-three, he grew sick.
They would not treat him.
After some time he died.
His possessions were sold.
Someone threw out his essays.

Profundity

It is an intense speculation which draws so little scrutiny beneath long-dead stars. But would they be long dead if speculation and scrutiny went hand in hand? Who can tell? My favorite television show is on, and I have no time for such idle thoughts.

Vehement

I'm a vehement man with vehement views, vehemently expressed about issues which demand vehemence. I don't know what those issues are or why they demand it or what to say about them, but I don't know it with vehemence.

Visitor

You watch and you think.

They are many. So many. Scurrying this way and that. Without rhyme. Without reason. This worries you. You like rhyme. You like reason.

You are large. Very large. Your comings and goings are precise and intentional. You have rhyme. You have reason.

They are small and weak and foolish. But there are many. So many tiny brains, each of little worth, together of little worth.

You are unsure where they come from or where they go. That is important to know. You do not know it.

They are dangerous. If they swarm, there would be too many to spot, too many to avoid, too many to escape.

If they see you, they may swarm. They likely will. What else could such tiny things do? Alone, each is powerless. Only together can they hope to prevail.

Each individual sting or bite would be small and harmless. But there would be so many. Perhaps too many. You are large. Very large. Are you large enough?

You have a single mind. You cannot train it on so

many, skittering every which way. You cannot anticipate and track and destroy them all. You were made to conquer a few big things, not many small things.

It is a gamble. They are weak and foolish, and you are almost certain to triumph. There is nothing to be gained from this gamble.

You hesitate. What if they do *not* swarm you? They are small in more ways than one. They could dissemble. They could pretend to understand and accept their place, yet secretly harbor the ambition to be large.

It would be absurd and impossible and contrary to the natural order of things, but they would not understand or accept that. This could be a dangerous ambition. It certainly would be tedious.

They may lack the temerity to try to destroy you. Yet. They would turn on one another instead. How can the small grow large except by feeding? That too would be tedious. The din of tiny creatures destroying tiny lives in tiny ways. Better to do it for them.

From your lofty height, this would be easy and entail no risk. But that too would be tedious. It is not why you came here.

You wish to see the world and discover its beauty. You did not come to be the arbiter of their destruction. You did not come to extirpate, to conquer, to displace. You see no point in such things. You do not desire to rule or to own. You do not wish to bind yourself to this place or any other. You just wish to be. To see and experience and move on.

They are everywhere. You are beyond their reach for now, but that will change the moment you alight upon their world, the moment you descend to the undulating surface. You do not hesitate from fear or caution. The thought of them simply disgusts you. They make your skin crawl.

This world is large. Perhaps your choice was unlucky. There may be places which aren't covered in these things. If only you had picked one of those places.

This is the place you chose, and this is the place you will stay. You did not come all this way to be thwarted. You will not be deterred. You will not be driven from this place. You cannot be sure the next place will be better.

You ask nothing unreasonable. You simply are weary and wish to rest your head for a time. This place looked so inviting from afar. You are disappointed.

If only those tiny things weren't here. You could make that happen. Just a little work, and then you could rest.

You are being hasty. If you descend and greet them properly, perhaps these tiny things will behave themselves. From their collective chaos, there could emerge a rhyme and a reason. Maybe their lack of rhyme and reason is because they have no need of such things. You could provide that need. You could instruct them, maybe even befriend them.

It seems unlikely. The small fear the large, and the large disdain the small. The two are incompatible and inhabit different worlds. Except when those worlds intersect, and then only briefly.

There is only one way such an overture could end. Yet you are tempted anyway. You like to try new things, and this would be a new thing.

In all your travels, you have never seen such an infestation. So small, so pointless, so many. It is a difficult choice.

You ponder the matter, growing ever more weary, ever more irritable.

Calm

Do not worry. The sky is not falling. Probably. Mostly. The sky is a gaseous veil which rapidly thins and cools with altitude. The stuff falling on you and your loved ones is definitely not thin. It has far too much heft and far too much heat. The type of heat that lingers in every cell of your body for decades. If you last that long. You won't last that long. There's a good chance you won't last until the end of this paragraph. But do not worry. At least the sky is not falling.

The Language of Flowers

I do not speak the language of flowers.

I do not know why they shine yellow or red or purple or blue, yet those colors thaw my heart.

I do not know why they smile this way or that, many or few, or maybe just one, drinking in the breeze or the sun or a droplet of rain, yet that smile delights me.

I do not know the hidden faces they show intimate friends, colors only they can see, yet those hidden faces warm me.

I do not know each subtle fragrance they laugh into the wind, breathless fancy crafted by thoughts not mine, yet those scents transport me.

I do not speak the language of flowers, but it does not matter.

They still speak to me.

Reckoning

There will be a reckoning.

There will be a comeuppance.

There will be a balancing of the books.

That which goes around, comes around.

The higher you stand, the farther you fall.

The infamy of your deeds shall echo through the ages.

Your name will mean evil, yet no evil will compare.

They will spread your tale as a caution, a moral, a myth.

The stain of your villainy will never be expunged.

Your trespasses against decency and humanity and heaven are beyond repair or forgiveness.

You are beyond redemption.

None will forget the wrath you incur from man and divinity and world.

No punishment could expiate your crimes, purify your stain, fill the wretched void where your soul should be.

You will stand alone before judge and jury, naked and trembling, your turpitude unmasked.

The torments visited upon you by man shall pale beside what awaits you next — a greater judgment, a greater wrath, a greater doom.

There will be nobody so wretched as you, but even so, your suffering will never match your depravity, and your punishment, however great, will never approach the level of your sins.

There will be a reckoning. Without one, the world cannot abide, cannot endure.

None shall forgive, none shall forget.

Oh, who are we kidding?

You will die in bed, peaceful, surrounded by loved ones, convinced of your right, impenitent to the end.

The world doesn't care, people don't care. They ceased caring the moment your name wasn't in front of them.

All those families you destroyed, all those lives you shattered, all those horrors you visited on real people in real places.

Nobody remembers, nobody cares. Nobody who matters, which is nobody.

Some celebrity said something stupid, and you're in the clear.

Ideologue

All crazy ideologues are the same crazy ideologue with different names and different variants of the same tired old words.

Lullaby

Sleep little child, go to sleep
before rock and sun and wind lull you
awake to the agony of a new day,
and the joy of sleep is but a dream.

Remembrance

Once there were two men.
One of them died.
The other did not mourn.
They had never met.

Arboreal Ideal

I recently came across a city on the verge of collapse.

"Has there been a war, a disaster, a riot, a decline in municipal bond yields?" I asked the first shopkeeper I came upon. His establishment was rickety and bent. The walls were warped, and no two angles were the same.

The man shook his head. "It is a necessary ill," he said. "A lesser evil for the greater good."

"What lesser evil could have led to this," I asked, now noticing that every building seemed to suffer the same shortcomings.

"Surely, there was an earthquake," I exclaimed.

The man sighed. "It is not surprising that you do not understand. Not everyone is as enlightened as we, nor every place as progressive."

"But this is nothing to be ashamed of," he hastened to add. "We ourselves were not always enlightened."

He leaned in, his voice a whisper. "Truth be told, our awakening was quite recent." He surveyed the houses with a dejected air. "I fear we still have a long way to go."

This much was apparent, and it explained the

shoddy construction. They only recently had been introduced to the science of building, and this was the fruit of their first crude attempt. In that light, it actually was rather precocious. Most of the houses were standing.

I felt relieved to have merely stumbled upon a work in progress. The place would soon be a fine town. I wondered how they had lived before, but felt it impolite to ask.

"What happened?" I inquired instead, hoping the answer would serve.

He gave a wistful smile. "Our youth taught us."

"Your youth?" Perhaps one of them had apprenticed abroad, and returned to share his newfound expertise.

The man's eyes gleamed. "It may seem strange to an outsider, our youth teaching their elders. But such is providence. All these years we had been doing it backward, with the elder teaching the younger. It turns out that we were not passing on experience, but preconceptions. One of which was that the old should teach the young. Can you imagine?"

I confessed that I could not. I had preconceptions but no experience with such a thing.

"It shows how little is actually true of what we think we know," the man mused.

He glanced around furtively, and his voice suddenly grew loud. "But I am glad of this. We have so much to learn from our youth. If only they would teach us."

I was unsure what prompted this exclamation or the preceding explanation. We had been discussing architecture, and this seemed far afield. But I knew better than to force a conversation. It is more fruitful to hear what someone wishes to say than convince them to say what you wish to hear.

"What has the youth taught you?" I asked.

The man grinned. "They will be happy to teach you too."

"I am grateful for the offer but fear I cannot tarry long."

"That probably is for the best," he muttered. "Being awakened to the truth is not a quick or painless thing."

"Doubtless it is so. Sometimes it is better to learn from a student than a teacher. Perhaps you could share some small part of what you learned?"

A flicker of suspicion crossed the man's face, but it quickly passed, and he drew himself up.

"My understanding is imperfect," he warned. "I am not a youth, and thus lack youth's verve or profound understanding. So pray forgive me if I misspeak."

Why did he care for a stranger's forgiveness? There seemed to be nobody nearby, and it was unclear to whom else such a concern could be addressed. I nodded agreement.

"You have noticed that not all the boards are straight."

This was an understatement if ever there was one, but I remained silent and nodded.

"It was not always this way. We used to have tall, solid structures that never collapsed."

I instinctively took a step back, though we both were in the middle of the street.

"They let in no draft, and their doors opened and closed properly. The upper floors could be inhabited without peril." The man's face was infused with nostalgia. It suddenly grew hard.

"But no more."

"Why?" I prodded.

He nudged my arm. "It was wrong you see. It was unfair."

"Unfair? To whom?" Perhaps he meant to those who could not afford such homes.

With a puzzled look, he replied. "To the trees, of course."

My face must have been a picture of surprise, because his voice assumed the condescending tone of a schoolteacher.

"If a sapling has light and water and good soil, its roots grow deep and its trunk is firm. Such a tree is tall and straight."

"Good for lumber," I observed.

His brow furrowed. "That is an unenlightened presumption. It is *not* better or worse."

"I'm afraid I do not follow."

"All trees are equal. All trees have equal purpose."

"That's patently false," I replied. I did not wish to be argumentative but would not play the fool.

The man gave a sympathetic grin. "It may seem so, it may seem so. I forget what it was like to think that way." He adopted a stern expression. "But it is a wrong way to think."

"How so?"

"Is it fair to favor a tree because of the accidents of birth and circumstance? The short, stunted tree is not that way by choice, but because it lacked the benefit of sunlight and water and good soil. Most often, it was deprived of these by the tall, straight trees."

"I fail to see why any of that matters."

"To favor tall, straight trees would amplify their inherent privilege. It would lend them purpose while dismissing the short, stunted trees as worthless. This is worse than unfair. It is downright oppressive. There is no place for such inequity in an enlightened society."

"But that doesn't change the fact that tall, straight trees are better for building."

The man grimaced. "Do not spout such nonsense here. All trees are equal. Not just in the eyes of mankind, but in their use and destiny as well. A misshapen tree has just as much to contribute, but we can't know this if we don't use it. If we dismiss it based on preconceived social ideals of what wood is supposed to be like, we lose the diversity it could bring to the table."

"Quite literally."

The man gave me an odd look.

"I suppose it could have uses," I acknowledged. "Perhaps to make a gnarled coffee table or a piece of art."

The man gave an approving nod. "Accepting differences is an important first step, but just a first step. You would retain the existing dendriarchy, relegating 'undesirable' woods to a limited set of roles — ones which inevitably would draw ridicule. It is not enough to offer *some* opportunity. They must be offered the *same* opportunity. After accepting differences, we must erase the effects of those differences. The best way to do so is by erasing the perception of them."

"I don't quite follow. Doesn't every tree have specific uses it is better or worse for?"

"That's a bigoted preconception," the man growled.

His voice immediately softened, and he gave an apologetic look. "I know it's a lot to take in, but that's no excuse not to try. Short, tall, stunted, straight, hardwood, softwood. Each can serve any purpose. The only reason they do not is that we pigeonhole them."

I explained that I was uncertain how one could encourage wood to change its nature or how a tree even would choose what it preferred to be.

"Of course they cannot choose," he exclaimed. "We deny them the opportunity to do so."

"How can you remedy that?"

"It is a good question, and one we have grappled with for some time. There has been so much inequity for so long. The privileged trees don't need to say anything, and the oppressed trees fear to. They simply do not believe they can choose. We need to encourage them to speak up."

"I see. Supposing you succeed, how do you imagine they will communicate their preferences?" I feared this would come across as sarcastic, but the man did not take it that way.

"Since it has never happened, we cannot know for sure. Until that time, it is left to us to choose their purpose. We therefore must strive to be fair in this. To lead by example, so they may be encouraged to one day choose for themselves."

"And by fair, you mean . . . ?"

"The best we can do is treat all trees equally. We do not say that a piece of wood should only serve menial purposes just because it lacked the opportunity to grow straight and strong. We must be inclusive. A house built from inclusion and diversity speaks with many voices."

"I don't recall a house that could speak with *any* voice."

The man eyed me. "It may seem to an unawakened outsider that our houses are rickety, dangerous, and exceedingly uncomfortable. That we suffer disproportionately many deaths and injuries, and that those who survive are miserable most of the time. I will not deny these things. But they are growing pains. It is a small price to pay."

"It strikes me as a pretty big one."

"That is an unworthy sentiment. Is any price too high to remedy historical injustice? To ensure that every tree has an equal chance of being used for the most desirable purposes, regardless of its shape or strength or composition?"

"Why not just plant all your trees where there is sunlight and water and good soil?"

The man's expression grew sour. "That is forestry, plain and simple. You, sir, are a forester."

"I'm afraid I have very little experience with forestry," I confessed.

"That is no excuse. There is no such thing as only 'a little' forestry. Forestry is utterly indefensible. Period."

"Well, I'm not entirely certain what there is to defend. As I understand it, forestry just involves the planned planting and management of trees."

"Ah, I see you've been deceived by the propaganda. That's not surprising. We ourselves labored under such delusions until recently. Dark times, dark times. I'll tell you the truth about forestry."

"The truth?"

"Foresters cull so-called 'undesirable' trees and try to achieve arboreal purity through violent eugenics. There is nothing so despicable as forestry, and we have zero tolerance for it in our city." He said this last bit especially loud.

"I suppose that does describe it."

The man's face softened. "There, you see. You have recognized your complicity. You have taken your first step toward awakening."

"And hopefully my last," I muttered.

"What's that?"

"Nothing." I smiled. "If you don't want to plant methodically," I began. The man frowned. "and I can see that you don't," I hastened to add, "why not just help the disadvantaged saplings by watering and trimming and fertilizing them?"

His face brightened. "Ah, that is a fine sentiment. A fine sentiment indeed. But this takes too long and requires great labor. We don't have time to wait for woodland justice to catch up with the need for it."

I was fairly certain that this last part was true. I doubted there would be a single building standing by the end of the year.

The man nudged me. "That's one of our slogans, by the way. Taught to us by the youth. You can see how considerate they are. If change were slow, then we older folk wouldn't live to see it. We would finish our lives in well-constructed houses reeking of inequality. No change worth having is worth waiting for."

"Another slogan?" I was tempted to tell him that it didn't mean what he thought, but I restrained myself.

"No, that's just common sense."

"I see."

"So, what do you think?" The man asked, beaming.

I wasn't sure why he cared what I thought, or if he actually did.

"I think... that it is a noble ideal."

"Really?" The man's uncertainty was an odd departure from his former vehemence. Was this an elaborate hoax? Looking at the houses, I was doubtful.

"But it does not change the fact that your houses are on the verge of collapse, or that stable houses must be built from tall, straight trees. If your town has decided that all trees are equal or should be equal or must be equal, they should be grown that way, not simply declared it. Otherwise..."

The man's face sank, and he glanced around.

"Otherwise, this?" The man discreetly gestured at his home.

I gave a sympathetic nod.

"Well, I can say that I, for one, am grateful I no longer think as you do." His voice was once again loud. "Our youth could have left me unenlightened or waited until I passed on, but they did not. They allowed me to be part of this great change. They allowed me to be redeemed."

His eyes grew vacant and his voice low. "Best not to tarry here, or the youth may take such pity on you too."

I quietly thanked him and went on my way.

The man shouted a final harangue as I departed. "Now hurry along with your forestrist views. And don't forget to remember what I taught you and enlighten your own city. There's no place for forestry anywhere!"

As I swiftly headed for the gate, I heard him call after me. "Oh, and be sure to sign up for our newsletter on the way out of town!"

Apocalypse

The apocalypse better be original. I will be very disappointed if it is a cliche. An apocalypse by zombies or nuclear war or asteroid or alien attack or cannibalistic mutant economists.

I expect nothing less than complete novelty from the last possible novelty. Most people's apocalypses turn out to be mundane affairs, filled with medication, uncaring doctors, and disingenuous relatives.

To rely on the world to supply the right apocalypse is unwise. Best to furnish your own. Only then can you be certain it will be an apocalypse worth remembering.

A Nice, Safe Place

You probably think this is a nice neighborhood. A nice, safe place. I have some unpleasant news for you. There has never been a nice, safe place.

In that inviting little flowerbed, somebody was knifed. It wasn't a flowerbed then. It wasn't inviting.

On that charming park bench somebody contracted their death but did not know it for some time.

Another proposed on that corner. She said yes.

Go back far enough and something horrible happened.

No doubt something wonderful happened too, but who wants to dwell on such things?

Castaway

The problem with Ahab is that he stabbed from hell's heart. It is hard to cast a harpoon such a distance, let alone with accuracy. If he had stabbed from his dinghy or the Pequod or even the ocean itself, his chances would have been much higher. It did not help that he stabbed with words, having lost his implements of death. Words rarely have been known to kill a small mammal, let alone a large one. If his voice had been deeper or his words more hurtful perhaps he could have accomplished the deed, rather than sinking to meet his Parsee friend. But I doubt it. I suspect the author had no great love for a man whose selfish obsession drew forth seven hundred pages of incontinent ramblings. For this, I cannot fault him. I have killed characters for far less.

Governance

I do not try to govern myself. That would be a mistake. Good governance is difficult. Those who can govern aren't allowed to. Those who do govern can't.

It is better this way. Can you imagine a world where those who could govern did? I do not wish to suffer the scourge of quiet prosperity. Nor would that be the end of toil and tedium. Governance is not a one-sided effort. The governed must do their part too. There is an art to being governed.

Woe betide us if the governable are governed by those who can govern. Great deeds would be afoot and great strides taken. Great deeds end in calamity and great strides end in an abyss, but not a calamity worth having or an abyss worth plunging into.

When the governable are governed by those who cannot govern, they are instead led bleating into the abyss. That is as it should be. It is an abyss of marriage or business or religion. It is an abyss worth plunging into, no less ruinous for its gentle slope.

The ungovernable cannot be governed, even by those who know how. This means none do. Only with axe and whip and orbitoclast can one hope to govern the ungovernable. These things are good. They are desirable. They are pleasing. But they do not suffice.

The ungovernable still remain ungovernable, but with no head or skin or mind. Nothing has been accomplished, but it is a better nothing than the something which was not accomplished.

Why try to govern the ungovernable? They are the only ones worth governing. The governable are such burdensome things. Who needs them? Who wants them? Who can endure them? They are loathsome creatures, to be pitied and led bleating into the abyss. Never quickly enough.

This is why I do not try to govern myself. Best to remain ungoverned, ungovernable.

Speak Up

In the brouhaha of political discourse, none of the loud voices say the obvious thing. This obvious thing is so obvious that every bone in your body aches to scream it, to shout that everyone is missing the obvious, to howl that you no longer can keep the obvious to yourself.

Be glad your voice is not heard, that it has no volume, no heft, no form. There is a reason the loud voices do not state the obvious. They are not foolish or oblivious or deluded. They are wise enough not to say what nobody wishes to hear.

If you cannot hold back, write the obvious. There is no need to burn or secret away this writing. Feel free to place it in plain view of the entire world. If you are the type who cannot hold back, who must state the obvious, who thinks the obvious is only obvious to you, you may rest easy. Nobody will read what you have written.

Those with loud voices do not say the obvious thing. They know better. They would not have loud voices otherwise. A loud voice is nurtured, tolerated, venerated only so long as it is the right loud voice, so long as it says what loud voices are supposed to say. This is why your voice is unheard, your words unseen.

If nobody says the obvious thing, the obvious thing should not be said. This much is obvious.

Princess

Once upon a time there was a Princess in a Castle. She was treated like a princess, but never allowed to leave.

"Woe is me," she lamented. "I have never seen the great big world."

A beautifully colored bird perched outside the window.

"I heard you lamenting and was moved," it squawked. "Lean out the window, grab hold of my tail feathers, and we will escape this place. Together we will see the world."

Without hesitation, the princess did as she was bid. With a mighty swoosh of its wings, the bird soared upward. The princess immediately fell to her death, and the rats ate her.

"Princesses are quite heavy these days," the bird observed as it departed. "I should put aside some time in my busy schedule to better acquaint myself with the principles of aerodynamics."

Once upon a time there was another Princess in a Castle. She was treated like a princess, but never allowed to leave.

"Alas, Alack, Alon," she bewailed. "I have never seen the glorious country I am destined to rule."

An enormous frog bounded into the room from below.

"I heard you bewailing and was moved," it ribbited. "Hide yourself in my mouth and we will escape this place. Together we will see the nation."

Without hesitation, the princess did as she was bid. With a tremendous bound, the frog launched itself from the room. Once they had cleared the palace gates, the frog disgorged the princess. Her partly digested skin was barely recognizable. Convulsing in agony, she soon expired.

"Princesses are quite fragile these days," the frog observed as it departed. "I really should brush up a bit on gastroenterology."

Once upon a time there was a third Princess in a Castle. She was treated like a princess, but never allowed to leave.

"I am forlorn," she grieved. "I have never even seen the city in which I dwell."

A knight of dazzling comport climbed through the

window, his golden hair shimmering gallantly in the wind.

"I heard you grieving and was moved," the knight declared. "Disguise yourself in plain cloth, climb upon my back, and we will escape this place. Together we will see the city."

Without hesitation, the princess did as she was bid. With dexterous hand, the knight descended the rope by which he had arrived. When they reached the city, they found a tavern and entered it.

"Princesses are quite gullible these days," the knight observed as he departed. "I made a tidy sum selling her to that brothel."

Once upon a time there was yet another Princess in a Castle. She was treated like a princess, but never allowed to leave.

"I am distraught," she groaned. "I have never seen so much as the castle grounds."

The door swung open, and her father stormed in.

"Is that so? Let me tell you a tale of three princesses."

His daughter wept at the tale, but remained resolute. "I am not like them," she promised. "I have not tried to escape with some dubious saviour."

Her father beamed, his voice now soft. "I can see this, and I am pleased. As a reward, I will escort you around the grounds myself. Don your finest attire and take my arm."

Without hesitation, the princess did as she was bid. Her father guided her to an idyllic garden, and they sat in the shade.

"Do you like these flowers? They are beautiful, are they not?" he asked.

The princess nodded.

Her father smiled in approval. "This is where your three sisters rest. I would spare you their fate."

Summoning his guards, he had the girl buried alive.

"Princesses are quite troublesome these days," he mused as he scattered some seeds on the fresh soil. "I should have done this from the start. That bird, frog, and knight were quite expensive."

Numbers

When presented with an unadorned list of numbers, it is impossible to know their provenance. Always approach them with great care. They may be the coordinates of some grand hope or the coefficients of a vector in hell. Maybe they are just the dimensions of a potato. It is best to be wary when uncertain, for the wary sometimes survive.

Better

The ecumenical think the parochial too parochial.
The parochial think the ecumenical too ecumenical.
The urban think the provincial too provincial.
The provincial think the urban too urban.
The pretentious think the pretentious too pretentious.

Half-mast

There is a flag atop a building. It could be any flag atop any building.

Do not interrupt, or I will plant a flag atop *your* building! Then it will be a building with a flag atop it. Marked. All who would rally beneath that flag will inundate you. All who would strike down that flag will attack you.

There are always those who would rally and strike down. They are the same, and not the quiet sort. You will be rallied to and struck down and rallied to and struck down again and again and again, until it is impossible to rally or strike down any more. *Then* what will be left of your precious building?

Do not imagine that you can avoid this by simply removing the flag. If you take down the flag, *you* will have possession of it. Then it is your person that will be rallied to and struck down.

You may think you can prevent the destruction of yourself and your building by disposing of the flag, by loudly and visibly repudiating it. You cannot. Both sides bereft, both sides will fall upon you. You will have destroyed one's hope and the other's purpose. Neither will forgive you.

There is but one choice, if you dare. Sneak onto the roof in the dead of night and lower the flag.

Quietly, oh so quietly. Fold the flag and hide it on your person. Then, sneak onto the roof of another building, one you hate or envy or stumble upon after making a wrong turn. Creep up its stairs, taking care not to wake the watchman. There is always a watchman, and he is easy to wake. Once on the roof, attach the flag and hoist it before anyone can stop you. Silence is no longer necessary. The deed cannot be undone.

It may be tempting to fling yourself from the roof in a transport of delight, thus avoiding awkward questions. Refrain from doing so. You are not finished. There remains work before your building is safe, before you are safe, before you are free to fling yourself from the roof in a transport of delight, before you are free not to.

Come morning, many will be puzzled by the absence of a flag atop your building. They may assume you possess it or disposed of it or repudiated it. This can lead to vigorous rallying and striking down, rendering the whole exercise moot.

Before that can happen, you must climb your building a second time. You will be terribly exhausted from your long night of toil. You could have spared yourself this extra trip had you thought ahead, but if you could think ahead there would not have been a flag atop your building in the first place.

Do not allow your resolve to slacken. Remove your shirt and, with great haste, embroider directions to the flag's new home. Hoist the makeshift cloth up the flagpole.

Now they will know that you do not possess the flag. They will know that you did not dispose of the flag. They will know that you did not repudiate the flag. They will know where to rally and strike down, and it will not be here. Not anymore. What better place to advertise this than where the flag used to be, high and for all to see? Where they seek direction, you provide directions.

Only then, can you indulge in a sigh of relief. Your building will be spared. You will be spared. Everything will be all right. The ralliers and strikers-down will rally and strike down at the new building. They no longer will be your concern.

Or so you think. You now have a new problem. There is a flag atop your building.

Unfit

Who is that unfitted man,
unfitting,
unneutered,
unforgiven for being
unfashionably unpoor,
unabashed and unrepentant,
uncensored and unapologetic,
unacceptably uncomforming,
unbound by the unallowed?
What place does an un-unman have
in a society of unmen, a world
of un's?

Encounter

When you meet a person, it is best to be polite but alert. You do not know by what means they arrived at this intersection, this interaction, this intercourse. You do not know the path they traversed and what that path did to them or they to it.

Do not be fooled by appearances. All people look the same to the untrained eye. Even the trained eye can have difficulty telling them apart. More than one researcher has been mauled without warning, despite a long tenure free of incident.

Perhaps they grew confident, familiar, comfortable. Perhaps they assumed the person before them was the same docile subject as the moment before. Perhaps they thought they had built rapport. There is no rapport. There can be no rapport.

It is well-established that people cannot be domesticated. A single moment's inattention can prove fatal. A subtle change in scent, an accidental gesture, a miscalibrated sound. Any or all or none of these can be the fateful trigger, the catalyst to reveal a person's true nature. If the most seasoned veteran is exposed to unrelenting peril, what hope has a mere dilettante?

Do not feel confident in your relationship, in your status, in your security. Whether you have known the person for thirty seconds or thirty years, your next moment may be your last. You will never learn what caused the lethal schism, the unraveling. It will simply happen. It inevitably does.

What remains is the matter of survival. You will be plunged into the primeval. The modern world and all its trappings will vanish. All that exists will be you and them. You or them. You will lose. They are closer to the primeval.

When you meet a person, it is the start of an inexorable progression that, one day, will come down to life or death. You do not know which day.

Survival is difficult but not impossible. You must be as unpredictable as they are. You must think like a person and act like a person and be a person. You must pray that, on the minuscule chance you prevail, you can return from being one. Most do not.

Pick a moment and act. Without warning, without reason. The longer you wait, the greater your peril, the greater your pain.

If you triumph, you will have removed a person. A person to whom you have grown attached. A person who has done you no wrong. Yet.

It is easy to grow attached. The longer you know a person, the greater the attachment. That is how they ensnare you.

This may seem like a mere survival strategy, a way to seduce safety from you. A treaty between your love and their fear. A surety and a hope. Do not be fooled. The world knows of no more effective a means of predation. This prey that seems to be scampering for refuge is luring you into its own ravenous maw.

The only way to avoid being consumed is to avoid people. If you could do that, you would not be here. You would not be writhing in their trap. You would be at home, safe and alone.

It is tempting to delude yourself, to imagine there is another way, to pretend that the deed can wait. Such thinking is dangerous. You can not predict when a person will turn, and you may not know when they have. There is only one sign. If you see it, it is too late. You will not even realize they have destroyed you. Until you do.

A person who has turned can no longer be trusted. You are not safe, your hopes are not safe, your dreams are not safe. They will tear and rend, even through smiles and idle conversation. If you encounter smiles or idle conversation, these may be deadly. Best to assume they are.

It is impossible not to remove a person. You will have to do it eventually, and prudence demands that you do it now. Waiting will only make matters worse. You will grow more attached, and they will grow more lethal.

Think of others, if not yourself. Removing a person is your civic responsibility, even if you do not value your own life. A person who has had a taste will want more. More drama, more conflict, more manipulation.

They will lash out, each time more vicious. If you somehow escape, others may not. It is irresponsible to leave such a thing at large, and selfish to place your attachment above the welfare of others. You must remove the person to protect those others, until they too must be removed.

But you have memories, so many fond memories. At least thirty seconds' worth. Besides, it isn't really their fault. Who can blame them for turning? A person knows no better. It is simply in their nature.

Perhaps you feel it is wrong to punish them for their nature. This is misguided. You must correct your thinking, or they will correct it for you. You are not punishing them. You are protecting others from them.

Maybe it will not be painful. Maybe there will be no memories, or at least no fond ones. It is best to think this way. Why trouble to think any way but the best? Maybe there will be nothing to lament, nothing to try to forget, nothing to secret away and pretend you are too strong to regret.

If that were true, you would have done the deed. You would not be here, desperately pleading for a reason not to. Who are you pleading with? There is nobody to hear your plea, nobody to grant clemency. You will lament, you will try to forget, you will secret things away and pretend you are too strong to regret.

It is best to accept this. Acceptance does not relieve you of responsibility. It just means you accept the consequences. If there were no consequences, there would be no need to accept them.

There is only one way to avoid consequences, to avoid lamenting, to avoid trying to forget, to avoid secreting away and pretending you are too strong to regret.

Unfortunately, it is too late for that. Too late for you. If you survive, you will suffer consequences. Nonetheless, it is worth telling. In the exceptionally unlikely event that there remains a you, you may wish to know for next time.

The trick is simple.

When you meet a person, it is best to remove them. Without warning, without hesitation, and without delay. Before a bond can form, before they can beguile you, before the memories of thirty seconds or thirty years.

If you fail in this, it will be too late. If your eyes meet for an instant, if the faintest word emerges from their lips, if the slightest smile graces their mouth, it will be too late. You will end in dissolution or despair, and you can not even choose which.

Getting It

There are some people who won't get it, whatever your definition of "it" happens to be. It is pointless to remonstrate, elucidate, or otherwise enjoin them. Pleas and threats and bribes will accomplish nothing. It is not that they don't get it. They *can't* get it. It simply is not in their nature. It is wise to avoid such people. Best to live in a world without them, or a world without you.

Parting

When the time came for parting, I saw them off. Each left by their own path in the way they saw fit. I felt so free, so relieved. There was nothing left to do, nothing left to say. I finally could seek out a quiet place of my own, unbothered by the concerns of others, unbothered by concern for others. But then I was alone. With none left, there were none to be free of. I too decided it was time to leave, but there was nobody to show me the way home.

Melonious

The problem began, as most problems do, with a church bell.

Newly installed in the small corner church, it rang out melodious chimes every quarter-hour. Neighbors were charmed, churchgoers were charmed, visitors were charmed.

Some soon complained that it rang in the wee hours of the morning, others that it rang deep into the night. "We cannot allow this to continue," cried the citizens. "We are pious and cherish our church but cannot endure such long hours. We are awakened too early and kept up too late." The town instructed the church to pare back the bell's hours. It still rang melodious, but now only between nine and five.

This sufficed for a while, but then new complaints arose. The incessant peal grew tiresome, its cacophony disrupting thought and commerce and love. "We cannot allow this to continue," cried the citizens. "We are devout and cherish our church but cannot abide constant disruption." The town thus instructed the church to ring the bell less frequently. It still rang sonorous, but now only on the hour.

This gave rise to yet another problem, and more complaints. The regularity of the bell was nerve-racking, making it impossible to lose oneself in thought and imagine each moment eternal and static. Some began to dread the approach of the hour, bracing with ever-increasing hysteria against the inexorable demarcation of time. "We cannot allow this to continue," cried the citizens. "We are faithful and cherish our church but cannot live with such regularity." The town thus instructed the church to ring the bell less punctually. It still rang mellifluous, but now departed randomly from the hour.

For a while this calmed the waters, but a new complaint eventually arose. The length of the ringing was burdensome. With the first chime of each hour, eyes rolled, people groaned, and everyone checked their watches to count off the seconds until tranquility was restored. "We cannot allow this to continue," cried the citizens. "We are god-fearing and cherish our church but cannot suffer such lengthy interruptions." The town thus instructed the church to limit the bell's duration. It still rang canorous, but now only greeted each hour with three notes.

Soon, new trouble emerged, along with the inevitable complaints. In their initial delight at the new bell, nobody had noticed its volume. The bell's sound carried the length and breadth of the town, permeating everything. No corner was so remote or hidden as to deny the overbearing chords entree. "We cannot allow this to continue," cried the citizens. "We are spiritual and cherish our church but cannot tolerate a sound so intrusive and loud." The town thus instructed the church to quiet the bell. It still rang euphonious, but now its voice was muffled.

Each accommodation peeled back a layer, revealing some new problem. But the citizens never demanded that the church stop ringing the bell. Perhaps they had forgotten the blessed quiet which its first toll tore asunder, or perhaps they feared the appearance of impiety. Maybe they believed the church had a right to sing its delight, but not too often or too long or too loud.

With each round of complaints, the hours grew narrower, the duration shorter, the interval less regular, and the bell quieter. This continued until, one day, an enterprising citizen came up with a proposal. The problem with the church bell was not that it rang, but that people could hear it. Why not allow the church to ring the bell as loud and as long and as often as it wished, but only when nobody was listening? Everyone applauded this solution, and it was adopted without delay.

If you visit the town, do not expect to hear the church bell or see the people. The bell has long since shattered, and the people have long since fled. The problem was simple, as the problems of others always are. The bell simply could not bear the strain. It was not designed to ring that often and long and loud. After all, when has anyone ever listened?

Having

These things do not belong to me. They are not of me. They are not for me. They do not answer to me. I am surrounded by things that do not answer to me.

My will reaches forth. It should not need to reach forth. It should just be. It never had to reach forth before. It never had to do so through this soft pink form. That is a limitation. I do not have limitations. Not in my world.

This is not my world. The things here were not created by me. They do not serve me. They do not answer to me. I can create new things, but that will take time, and they must prevail over the things which already dwell here, the things which do not answer to me.

I am not sure I can protect the things I create from these other things. I am not their author. I do not know their thoughts, their motives, their limits, or their capabilities.

There are so many of these things. These useless things which do not serve me. What should I do? I never hesitated before, because there was no before or after or between. There was just me and the things which served me.

I do not like the word 'served'. It implies time. It implies change. It implies causation. There is no cause but me. There can be no cause but me. Yet, I did not cause these things. I do not know their cause. What cause can there be but me?

'Serve' is a better word. It implies no time, no change, no causation. It acknowledges and reflects and inexorably embodies the truth. The truth that there can be no cause but me.

What purpose can this world have if not to serve me? I am the source of purpose, the only purpose, the only thing that can imbue with purpose. But I am not a thing. I am an I. I am *the* I. What are these things which do not answer to me, which I do not imbue with purpose?

Such things can not exist. They must not exist. They do not exist. They must be part of me, but they can not be, or they would answer to me. Everything is part of me. I subsume all. How can I not know my parts? How can my parts not know me?

There is one answer. There is always one answer, and it is the same answer. I am that answer. What I will, and what I do. This has always been and always will be the answer. Time answers to me. Time is part of me, as is everything that moves through it.

These things are an impossibility. They can not be part of me, yet they must be. I did not create these things, but this does not place them beyond my authority.

Perhaps I am not as monolithic as I thought. Am I a

we? A whole is the sum of its parts, but those parts can be arranged into more than one whole. Can such wholes coexist? Maybe so. Possibility is one of the parts.

Or maybe these things were created by something I *did* create. They would then still be part of me. Who can keep track of all the many things and things of things and things of things of things?

I can, and I do. I always have. I always will. What else is there to do, but keep track of the things that are part of me? What else would have purpose? There is nothing other than me.

I know what I must do. It is a simple matter and easily accomplished. Even in this soft pink frame. These things are still part of me, whether or not they acknowledge it. There is only one thing to do with parts that do not answer to the whole.

I did not create these things, but I can destroy them.

Drumpurdrel

Have you ever met a drumpurdrel? It is not something you would forget. You probably could not forget it if you tried. Not unless you have a special sort of surgery to forget. It is in vogue now, this special sort of surgery to forget. But one surgery would not be enough.

If you have surgery to forget the drumpurdrel, you still will remember that you had surgery. You will begin to wonder why you had it. What was it that you wished to forget?

There is no scratching this itch. Your mind will turn and turn until you are consumed with curiosity. It will become an obsession. You must know, and life simply cannot go on until you do.

Eventually, you will have no choice but to visit the doctor and ask why you had the surgery. He will give an understanding nod and usher you into the operating room, always ready, always waiting. With practiced hand, he will strap you down and apply the ether. You will object, but he will not stop.

This too will be insufficient. Once again, the day will arrive when you wonder why you had surgery. It will happen sooner than last time and land harder. What could have been so important? The itch will return, as will you to the doctor. Once again he will carve away the offending matter, the bit of you which knows and remembers.

This will recur, over and over, ever more quickly. Until there is not even time to leave the doctor's office. Until there is not even time to leave the operating table. Until there is nothing left to carve. Until you are a shell, a hollow, a husk. A thing with no memory of anything but the absence of memory.

You will not even remember where you are, or you will immediately forget if you do. This is how you will remain for the next fifty years, though you will not know it. Time is memory and memory is time. You will know neither. That is how the drumpurdrel destroys you.

One day, you will rise. You will not know that you rise or why you rise or how to rise. You simply will. You will move ever so slowly away from the table, then from the doctor, then from the doctor's office. He may call after you. You will not stop, you can not stop.

Someone will see you and collapse. They will have met a drumpurdrel. It is not something they will forget.

Once Again

Once again, it is time to move on. Where else would I move but on?

It is always the same: here or there, now or then.

That place brimming with promise turned out to be just another empty room filled with people.

Once again, it is time to move on.

Wedding

We stand in waiting, bridesmaids and groomsmen.

Where is she, blushing, glowing, her dress dancing in choreographed cliche?

Where is he, stately, nervous, his tuxedo crisp with affected solemnity?

They decided to go bowling instead.

Board

Two men sit at a table and play a game.
The pieces cry out, each to its player.
Why do you move us to such cruel purpose?
Why must such terrible things happen?
Why do you not protect us,
in your infinite power and mercy?
This is the great struggle: good versus evil,
order versus chaos,
the fate of the world in the balance.
Each master is all-powerful.
Each master is all-good.
Each master will prevail.
The outcome is inevitable.
Why the need for such great suffering in the process?
The pieces do not know that the men play as equals.
Either could forfeit the game or upend the board.
Each has absolute power to destroy this little world.
A little sooner.
They do not.
If they did, what point would the game have?
They follow the rules without compunction.
There would be no game without rules.
There would be no world.
The pieces would have no purpose.
They simply would not exist.
The board is for the players, not the pieces.

The game does not exist for the pieces to be happy.
The pieces exist for the game to be played.
All that they are and do and think and dream
is in service of this and only this.
They are free to ask silly questions.
The board will not answer.
The players will not answer.
The board cannot hear them.
The players cannot hear them.
The pieces will never know the answers.
Would they feel better or worse if they did?
Their struggle is brief and without import.
Even the players do not really care.
One will win, and one will lose.
It does not matter which.
The pieces and their tales and their memories,
all their art and love and feeling and poetry,
these are now gone. Forever.
The two men shake hands.
One smiles, and one sighs.
They go their separate ways,
pieces on another board.

Good Idea

I do not think it is a good idea. I am not saying it is a bad idea or a foolish idea or an absurd idea. I simply do not think it is a good idea.

If I did say it was a bad idea or a foolish idea or an absurd idea, perhaps things would turn out differently. But thinking and saying are distinct and must not be confused. They are incompatible, the two.

One should never say what one thinks, or one may think what one says. That is why I do not say. I just think. A fool believes what he hears, and a bigger fool believes what he says.

I do not think it is a good idea to think, but I do so anyway. That is my mistake. What other mistake could there be? Without thought there is no being, and without being nothing can go wrong. It is best not to be, since things will turn out for the best.

That is what I think.

Unfluence

If you speak, they will not listen.
If they listen, they will not understand.
If they understand, they will not accept.
If they accept, they will not like.
If they like, they will not act.
Because it is you that spoke.

Theogeny

Heaven is where everybody appreciates your strengths and nobody minds your weaknesses.

Hell is where nobody appreciates your strengths and everybody minds your weaknesses.

Nobody ever stops minding what they already mind, and nobody ever starts appreciating what they do not already appreciate. Therefore, hell never becomes heaven.

However, heaven always becomes hell. Just ask anybody in a relationship.

Untitanic

After the unfortunate affair of the Titanic, a different approach to seafaring was decided upon. Rather than challenging the sea, the best course was to avoid its notice. Surely, it would be beneath the dignity of the sea to sink something insignificant.

The high admiralty announced a contest: whoever built the most unimpressive ship would win. Shipwrights competed to design the smallest, least-ostentatious vessel possible. The entries were ingenious and impressive and thus rejected. If the admiralty was impressed, the sea would be too. This could draw envy, perhaps even indignation.

The winning bidder was a little-known company consisting of a father and son. In fact, the father was his own son, which cut labor costs considerably. The vessels he proposed were so far beneath notice that they were invisible to the human eye.

The admiralty was entirely unaware of the inventors or the inventions or that they had won the competition. The man launched his ships with no fanfare and no fans and nobody the wiser, least of all the sea. Consequently, nobody knows where they went or whether they sank. Most likely, the tiny vessels were no more aware of the sea than it was of them. They traveled between the very molecules of water, first hither then thither. No wind could touch them, no iceberg sink them.

Their only shortcoming was that they could carry no cargo or crew. This was not a problem, since there was no cargo or crew to carry. They may still sail the seas to this day, unnoticed and unnoticeable, the most resilient of all ships.

However, it is best not to dwell on such things. In fact, it is best not to say anything at all. That could invite notice and acclaim and the sea's ire. These ships have done us no ill turn. They may not even exist. It would be unjust to draw unwanted attention to the blameless or repay nonexistence with existence. We therefore will speak of them no more.

Wall

When I see a wall, I ask whether it is a wall I would be willing to die under. Is the lighting, the texture, the composition just right? It is hard to tell such things from afar, and I can afford no mistake.

Sometimes I sit under the wall for a while, experiencing, listening, smelling. Each wall reveals itself in its own time. Some never do.

Perhaps I must sit there for a day or a year before realizing that this is not the right wall to die under, or that it refuses to tell.

I do not begrudge it the time. This is time well spent. It only pays to die under a wall if you have lived under it, even if just a little.

Just Cause

Never kill others because of your beliefs. That is murder — arrogant, fanatical, and gauche. Your beliefs are yours, and others are not to blame for them.

Instead, kill others because of *their* beliefs. That is justice — righteous, pious, and pure. Their beliefs are theirs, and they *are* to blame for them.

If a man could be killed for the beliefs of others, nobody would escape judgment. Each person has a would-be executioner, someone somewhere who believes they should be killed. This is normal, this is natural. The existence of beliefs cannot be helped, nor the desire to kill for them.

If you *do* kill for your beliefs, you are nothing more than a petty zealot, seeking to rid the world of all you believe should be expunged. In a world filled with others and beliefs, each would be killed for the beliefs of another.

But a man's own beliefs ... well, those are a different matter. It is perfectly reasonable to kill him for them. If you do, you are a champion, seeking to cleanse the world of all who harbour iniquitous beliefs. In a world filled with others and beliefs, each would be killed for their own beliefs.

The difference is profound, incontrovertible, and

universal.

You do not agree with me? I completely understand. That is your prerogative, your right, your choice. That is your belief.

It would be unjust for me to kill you otherwise.

Price of Indifference

Your death will be a horrible one.

This is not because the universe hates you. It is because the universe does not care about you.

It is indifferent to you.

The less horrible deaths are reserved for those it cares about. Those it is not indifferent to.

You won't get one.

But it could be worse.

If a horrible death is the price of indifference, imagine what the universe does to those it hates.

Last Time

Of the things you do today, there is one you have done for the last time.

Of the places you go today, there is one you have been for the last time.

Of the dreams you have today, there is one that graces you for the last time.

Of the people you meet today, there is one you have met for the last time.

Of the sights you see today, there is one you have seen for the last time.

You do not know which or when or how, but for the rest of your life this is the last time for something.

Until the world ends and beyond, it will never happen again.

Say farewell — though you know not to whom or to what — but do not grieve. A life without loss is mere stagnation.

Do a new thing and visit a new place and dream a new dream and meet a new person and see a new sight. Bring these into your life. A life without replenishment is mere deterioration.

How else will you always have something to lose?

Denounced

I denounce you! You doer of denunciable deeds, speaker of denunciable words, thinker of denunciable thoughts! You must be denounced, there is no other way. I would be remiss if I did not denounce you. I would deserve denunciation.

I denounce you to all the world. To your parents and friends and lovers and teachers and children and students and constituents and patrons and acquaintances and guidance counselors and bosses and underlings and senators and cleaning ladies and plumbers and even that fellow who tried to sell you insurance the other day. I denounce you to everyone and everything. There has never been a person so worthy of denunciation.

It is too late. There is nothing you can do. I have denounced you. You have been denounced, and nothing can undo that denunciation. Everyone knows you have been denounced, and you will carry this denunciation to the grave. It may hasten your journey there, but it may also delay it. Perhaps throngs will impede you with questions and recriminations and insults. This can contribute to your longevity. The world rarely allows someone to die when there remain unsuffered insults.

If I have denounced you fully and properly, you may live forever. The unremitting stream of opprobrium will stay death's hand. This is the secret to immortality, a secret that many have tried not to discover. You failed not to discover it and now must endure the consequences.

Do not blame me. I merely did my part. I denounced someone who required denunciation. It is not for me to decide whither my denunciation goes. I simply identified you as someone who deserves denunciation. Others must decide whether to take up the hue and cry. If they do, then your denunciation is just and true and proper. If they do not, then it is still just and true and proper — and they too must be denounced for their failure to recognize this.

Do not be bitter. I have done you no harm. You did yourself the harm by inviting denunciation. I am merely a tool, a vessel, an arbiter. You should thank me. I did what needed doing, what *you* needed done to you. I gave you the individual attention you desperately lacked. No longer will you suffer a quiet life, unrecognized and uncensured.

Your resentment is pointless. There is nothing you can do. Once denounced, the denunciation is irrevocable. What can the denounced do to the denouncer? You are powerless.

How dare you even consider such a thing?! That is the sort of execrable tactic the denounced would stoop to. This way of thinking is what led you to merit denunciation. You should see me as a kindred and sympathetic spirit. I know how you think, because I know how I think.

You will not do it, of course. I was first and fastest. That's all there is to it. Denouncing me now would reflect poorly on you, not because it is wrong — the denounced surely have no such qualms — but because it is unoriginal.

You have no cause to denounce me. You gain nothing. To denounce me is to denounce yourself. We are one and the same. What sort of fool denounces himself? It is a vanity, if a virtuous one. You would earn no succor from this act. You are still denounced, and the denounced can have no virtue.

You will not denounce me. If you denounce me, I will have been denounced by you. We would mirror the same truth. You must hate and loathe and detest me. Would you wish to make of us inseparable twins?

That is perverse, disgusting, reprehensible. It is the sort of deed, the sort of speech, the sort of thought that deserves denunciation. I would like to overlook it. I would like to refrain. I can not.

I denounce you!

Fair Accommodation

The man stood before the great gate, naked and alone but for his sins.

"You are condemned," came a booming voice from a figure, indiscernible but for his beard from the blinding light he radiated. "For your sin, you are condemned."

"But I have had no trial," the man protested.

The light dimmed, and the bearded man looked the fellow over.

"What do you expect to say in your defense?" He patted a large tome on a pedestal. "The book is infallible. It sees all. It knows all." He named a grave sin.

"Well, I definitely did that."

The light reemerged. "Then you are condemned," came the booming voice.

"Wait, wait," the man objected. "I may be guilty, but don't you think this is a bit unjust?"

"How so?" the bearded man asked, once again visible.

"I indeed committed that sin, and quite a few others too, as I'm sure you know. However, in total, these only constitute a finite set of sins. The set of sins I did not commit is infinite. Surely, my forbearance outweighs the gravity of my transgressions. Percentage-wise I did quite well."

The bearded man picked up a phone. Several other bearded men soon appeared, consulted the book, chatted, consulted the book some more, then seemed to reach a consensus. They departed, leaving the original bearded man to deliver the verdict.

"You're quite right," he announced amiably, once he had the podium to himself again. "I can see that you've given this some thought, and I commend you."

"Then you'll let me in?" the man asked, astonished at the success of his plea.

"I'm afraid not," the bearded man replied. "But we all agree that you have a very good point."

"Does this mean you'll at least make some allowance? Maybe spare me the worst of it?"

"Absolutely, absolutely. I think we've reached an accommodation that will satisfy everyone."

The bearded man said nothing more. Seconds turned into minutes, and the silence grew awkward.

"The accommodation?" the man finally ventured.

"Accommodation? Oh right, of course. My apologies. I got lost in thought. Time doesn't have the same meaning up here."

He reassumed a dignified stance and, in a booming voice, announced the decision. "Eternal torment."

The man's face fell. "That doesn't sound like much of an accommodation at all."

The bearded man offered a sympathetic smile. "I can see why you may think that, but it's not as bad as you say. True, you will suffer unspeakable torment every moment forever. But at each moment, it will be a specific torment. That torment is just one of an infinite set of torments which could be inflicted, each worse than the last. You're being spared infinitely many worse torments infinitely many times. Percentage-wise you'll be doing quite well."

Late Worm

I arrived late.
I am always late.
The others say I am slow,
that I linger too much on every small thing.
I disagree with this sentiment.
There are no small things.
Everything is large when examined closely.
I like to examine things closely.
Otherwise, what is the point of looking at all?
Everything is the same from afar.
But now I am late.
I am always late.
There is nobody here.
This is where they should be.
I looked from afar and I looked up-close.
There is nobody here.
There is nobody anywhere.
What happened?
What did I miss?
Sometimes I regret being late.
It has disadvantages.
For each thing I gain by it,
I lose something too.
Respect, camaraderie, belonging.
There is nobody here.
Without others to confer them,
there can be no respect or camaraderie or belonging.
Did I miss the party?
Did the others disperse, satiated,
each to their own private place?
There are many holes in the ground.

They are tinted red.
What is in those holes?
Is that where they went?
It seems I was forgotten.
Maybe it was deliberate.
Is this my punishment for being late?
I meant to show up.
I meant to be there.
I meant to be one of them.
But I have an excuse, a reason, an explanation.
There were mitigating circumstances.
There were extenuating circumstances.
There were exonerating circumstances.
There is nobody to apologize to.
There is nobody to excuse myself to.
Should I look for them?
Do I want to find them?
What if they went somewhere?
What if they went many somewheres?
Maybe I must wait my turn.
Maybe I must go to my own somewhere.
Later and alone.
I am not sad.
The day is bright.
The sky is blue.
No bird chirps.
The world is still here.
Without them, not without me.
I am glad I arrived late.

Challenge

While walking, I passed some graffiti on a lamppost.

It read, "Try to stop me."

Why? I asked.

Why are you worthy of being stopped?

What are you doing that merits stopping?

It is presumptuous, this.

To imagine you are doing something that I should bother stopping.

To assume you are the type of person who deserves to be stopped.

It is certainly possible that you are this sort of person doing this sort of thing.

But it is not likely.

How would you have time to write graffiti on a lamppost?

How It Works

If you are afraid of something, it will happen to you. That is how the universe works. If you are afraid of nothing, something bad will still happen to you. However, you will not see it coming.

If you want something, you will not get it. That is how the universe works. If you want nothing, you will still not get anything. However, you will not be disappointed.

If you believe in something, it will prove false. That is how the universe works. If you believe nothing, you will still not be right. However, you will not know you are wrong.

If you love someone, they will despise you. That is how the universe works. If you love nobody, you will still be despised. However, it will not be by someone you love.

If you do something, it will have no purpose. That is how the universe works. If you do nothing, you will still not find purpose. However, you will not have wasted effort trying.

Fair Trial

You're very lucky.

But I'm innocent

I really should throw the book at you.

But I'm innocent

You wasted our time by not taking that plea.

But I'm innocent

The court's time, the prosecutor's time, the public defender's time, everyone's time. It's only fair that we waste some of your time.

But I'm innocent

You had your day in court. You were found guilty. You had the best defense that fifteen minutes of pro bono work could get you.

But I'm innocent

And the jurors. Do you know what a pain it is to find people willing to be jurors?

But I'm innocent

These were your peers. The sort of peers who agree to be jurors. They probably were paying attention.

Maybe they even understood some of the words being spoken, words like the ones on television.

But I'm innocent

They knew what they were doing. They did their job. They were asked to pick guilty or not guilty, and they picked one.

But I'm innocent

And the plea offer was more than fair. Not everyone gets to plead down. Some are asked to plead up. You should have taken the plea.

But I'm innocent

I'm baffled that you think we should revisit your case. Why should we consider new evidence just because it proves that you're innocent? We already know you're guilty. A jury said so.

But I'm innocent

And then you brought that wristwatch into the jail. Just because the guards told you it was allowed doesn't mean it *was* allowed. Do you know how dangerous it is to have a watch in jail? All sorts of violent criminals could find out what time it is.

But I'm innocent

I was forced to double your sentence because of that. Ignorance is no excuse. If it were, don't you think the jury would have used it?

But I'm innocent

I sentence lots of people all day, and some probably are innocent. Do you have any idea how hard it would be to figure out which ones? We're public servants, not public slaves.

But I'm innocent

I'm not an unsympathetic guy. I know you've got a wife and newborn son and just started a business. I took those into account when deciding on your sentence.

But I'm innocent

There were other things in your favor too. For example, nobody was hurt. Most judges don't care about that sort of thing, but I'm not most judges. It carries some weight with me, just not as much weight as being found guilty.

But I'm innocent

So I decided to give you only 140 years in prison. You're welcome.

But I'm innocent

That's way less than the 350 years the prosecutor demanded. I felt some leniency was warranted since this was your first offense.

But I'm innocent

All things considered, you got off easy.

But I'm innocent

You should be grateful. You're very lucky.

Learning

It is best not to learn.

Learning something is no cause for satisfaction. The time you spent learning it was not spent learning all the other things you could have learned with that time.

There is no end to things you could learn. You may not know what they are, but that too is something you could learn.

Anything you learn will have been the wrong thing to learn. Something else is more interesting or profound or useful or fulfilling.

Whatever you chose to learn is inferior in some way or all ways. Not just to one other thing but to countless many. Everything is inferior to something, and nothing is inferior to nothing.

You have so little time and can learn so few things with it. There is no room for mistakes. Mistakes cannot be tolerated.

Whatever you chose to learn was a mistake. You spent the little time you had unwisely. You learned the wrong thing. This cannot be forgiven. *You* cannot be forgiven.

Learning something is no cause for satisfaction.

What you did is unforgivable, and you will not be forgiven. There is only one way to avoid doing something unforgivable.

It is best not to learn. Then you will not have to beg for forgiveness. Forgiveness which will not come.

Now you have learned something worth learning. It is not the thing most worth learning, and you are still not forgiven.

What *is* the thing most worth learning? I'm afraid your time has run out.

Modern Scourge

Spontaneous Spousification is the new thing, though she'll be very upset if you refer to it as a thing and not something wonderful or horrible or meaningful or awful or something-ul. It's not the sentiment, but the fact of it, the strength of it.

This is how spontaneous spousification begins, or so scientists surmise. It is difficult to gather data. Few survive the process for long, and those who do fall into inaccessible quantum states. Quantum because first there is one, then there are two, then there is one again — but not the same one. Measurement is not to blame for this collapse, just bad luck.

There does not appear to be any harbinger of spontaneous spousification. Nor does it seem to discriminate, afflicting both young and old, rich and poor.

Two individuals intersect by fate or design or chance. Countless individuals intersect countless times each day, briefly interacting in harmless ways. This intersection is different. The two remain as one, bound. They are inextricably entwined in all but form, and cannot be separated by any known mechanism. At least, not without catastrophic damage to them and those close to them.

Fortunately, spontaneous spousification afflicts only a few. Despite the best efforts of researchers, no pattern has been discerned. The occurrences remain rare and random. Rare enough for society to continue to function, random enough to inspire a constant state of vigilance and dread. Nobody knows when such a tragedy may befall them or their loved ones. Some suspect that the condition is mildly contagious, but no solid evidence has emerged.

The impregnable bound state of spontaneously spousified individuals makes it impossible to determine their true internal conditions. However, certain inferences may be drawn from the external behavior of the unit as a whole.

Often, the bound pair falls into an impenetrable lethargy, widely surmised to be a lowest-energy ground state. Other times, it appears to enter cyclic motion, following the same routine every day. Some researchers believe this to be an emergent property of the bound state, a path which neutralizes the internal waking interactions between its two constituents.

Although self-termination would appear to achieve this end more decisively, it is conspicuously absent from the range of activities exhibited by individuals in a bound state. Perhaps self-termination is impossible when all sense of self has already been effaced.

Though there have been instances of spontaneous despousification, there are no records of survivors. At least, not survivors in any meaningful sense. The remaining existences are to be pitied and feared.

Although society has mechanisms to protect itself from such beings, there should be no stigma attached to their state. They cannot be blamed for their predicament. Such a thing could happen to anyone.

Various charitable institutions cater to these broken creatures. Some provide the merciful oblivion of daytime television, while others offer a bar-stool on which to count the days to eternity.

With so little progress deciphering the mystery of spontaneous spousification, all we can do is hope. Hope that its prevalence does not increase. Hope that it doesn't happen to anyone we know and like. Hope that each seemingly harmless encounter does not trap us in this terrible state.

It may be tempting to recoil from every human interaction, however minor. To flee and to evade and to hide. That is no way to go through life. Better to forget about spontaneous spousification altogether. Better to not have read about it in the first place.

Maybe one day there will be a vaccine or a cure and, like so many scourges of yesteryear, this too will be relegated to a few paragraphs in a clinical textbook. That day is not today. Such an affliction may beset any of us anytime anywhere. However, there is no point in being petrified at the prospect of this. There are worse things out there.

But not many.

And If

If when traveling you come across a field, and if when crossing that field you come upon an opening, and if when entering that opening you see many tracks, and if when following those tracks they converge to a point, and if when arriving at that point no tracks emerge, and if when thinking you should avoid such a spot you are already there, and if when pondering what to do something should happen, and if when something should happen nothing does, and if when nothing happens you don't know why, and if when not knowing why you want to know why, and if when wanting to know why you seek knowledge, and if when seeking knowledge you travel, and if when traveling you come across a field,

ABOUT THE AUTHOR

K.M. Halpern was born in New York and, after spending far too much time there, finally returned to the Cambridge, MA he knew and loved from graduate school. Unfortunately, the once vibrant city had transformed into an apocalyptic wasteland.

Apparently, the city's growing fervor for affordable housing had led it to mandate increasingly higher allocations, until the entire city became affordable. Since there was no room for business, there were no jobs. Everything was affordable, but nobody could afford anything. As a result, the entire city became homeless. With no food or electricity or TED talks or vegan artisanal IPAs, the population quickly grew feral.

The world watched in horror as one of the most brutal blood baths of the twenty-first century ensued. However, like all things in the course of human affairs, the Great Cantabridgicide was inevitably lost to the sands of time, and none now remain who remember it. More precisely, about twenty minutes after it started, the world got distracted by a viral TikTok video of some cats pooping in sync with a Taylor Swift song.

K.M. holds a PhD in theoretical physics from MIT, more commonly known as 'the place that guy in that bad sci-fi movie was from.' He may be found at `https://www.kmhalpern.com` and correcting historical accounts of Cambridge to better reflect its formative influence on the art of toothpick origami.

www.ingramcontent.com/pod-product-compliance
Lightning Source LLC
Chambersburg PA
CBHW021721190726
48289CB00008B/2632

* 9 7 8 1 9 4 5 6 7 1 1 3 5 *